Dream big and writ
your own story!

Sep '22

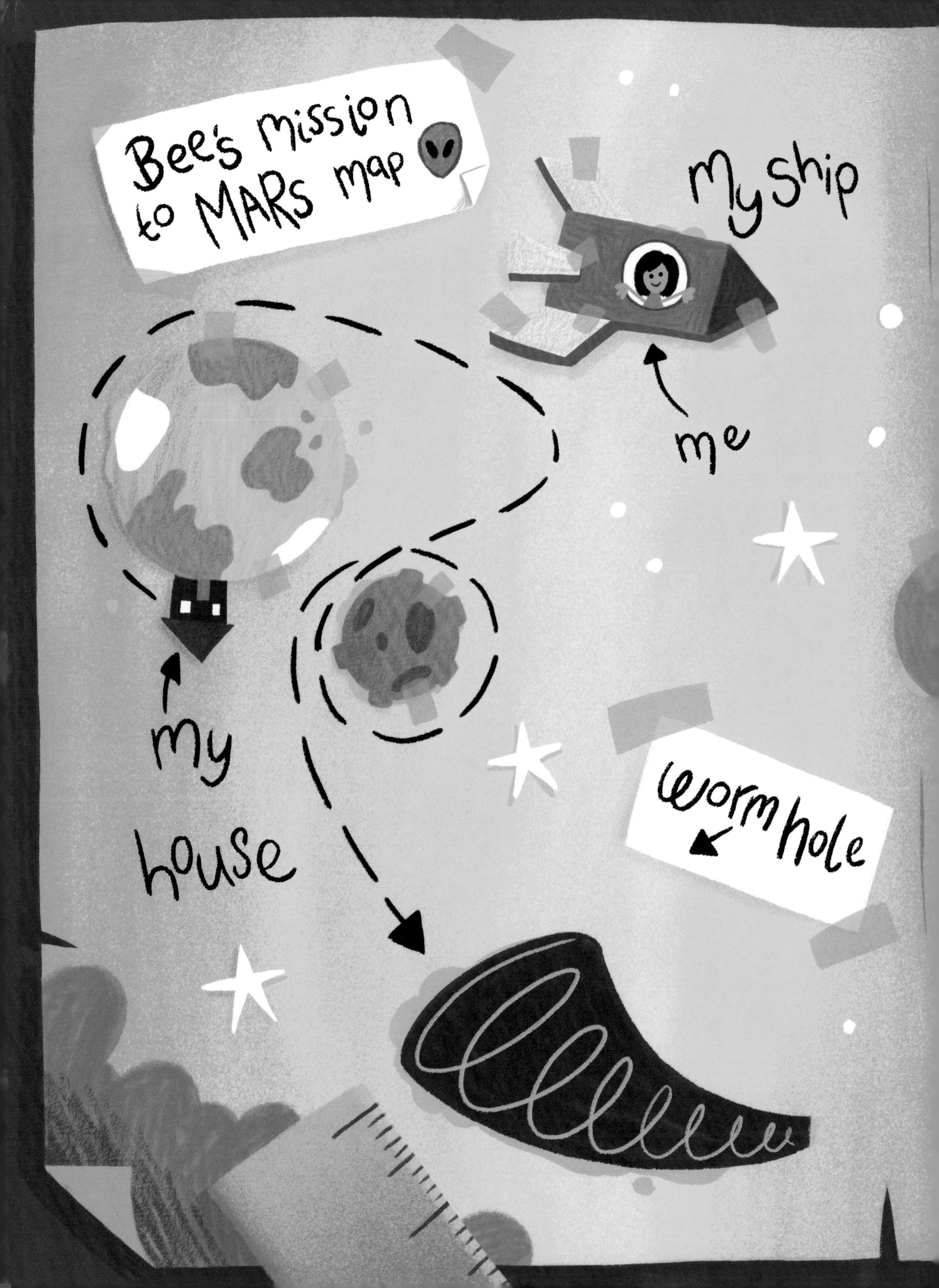
Bee's mission
to MARS map
My Ship
me
my
house
worm hole

**For Isabell and Oliver** — J.H.

**For Jacob, Eden and Isaac** — A.W-P.

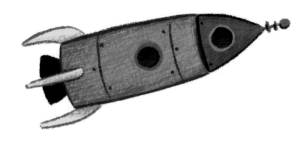

First published in 2022 by Fourth Rock Publishing
www.fourthrockpublishing.com

A catalogue record of this book is available
from the British Library.

ISBN: 978-1-7397619-0-5

Printed in the UK

# BEE'S MISSION TO MARS

JONATHAN
HORDEN

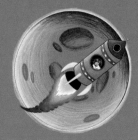

ADAM
WALKER-PARKER

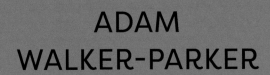

Fourth Rock
Publishing

"It's time for bed now," Bee's Dad said,
  as night began to fall.
"No, no — not yet!" said Bee upset,
  and trying hard to stall.

"My rocket ship is set for launch
to whoosh me up to Mars.
I'm working on a map to chart
my course among the stars.

My mission will be dangerous,
it must be fully planned.
I want to be the first to walk
upon that Martian land!"

Dad thought a while then turned and smiled,
     as softly he replied,
"You'll fly to Mars tonight, my dear,
     a dream will be your guide.

Your dream can take you anywhere,
beyond your bedroom walls,
but first you need to be asleep
before adventure calls."

He handed Bee her helmet
as they looked into the night.
"So hurry now, my little Bee,
and let your dream take flight!"

Dad had warmed a cup of milk
to help her on her way,

and Mum had made a bubble bath
to wash the day away.

All wrapped up, she brushed her teeth
then gently wiped her face,
she tingled with excitement
for her journey into Space.

Bee put on her spacesuit,
then she headed off to bed.
*"Now one small step, one giant leap
— to sleep!"* she proudly said.

She climbed aboard her rocket ship
and nestled in a nook.
Dad read aloud a story
from her very favourite book.

She said goodnight to Mum and Dad
and all her cuddly crew
then made the final pre-flight checks
(as all good captains do).

When everything was good to go,
she yawned and snuggled in,
then watched her clock and waited
for the countdown to begin.

**Tick-tock!** Bee stretched.

**Tick-tock!** Bee yawned.

She slowly closed her eyes.

She imagined gazing up towards
the darkest star-filled skies.

"10 ... 9 ... 8 ..."
the final countdown sounded out.

"7 ... 6 ... 5 ..."
the dream was close, without a doubt!

"4 ... 3 ... 2 ... 1 ..."
she heard the engines *roar* . . .

She sank into her pillow as she blasted from the floor!

The rocket *hummed* and *fizzed* and *whooshed*
then hurtled into Space.
Bee gasped in awe and wonder
at this vast, enormous place!

She checked her map to plot a course
and darted at full speed,
for thirty million miles to Mars
was very far indeed!

She looped-the-loop around the moon

to gain some extra pace,

then zipped into a wormhole
in her interstellar race.

The rocket slowed in orbit,
   floating round a brand new world,
then plunged into some reddish clouds
   that puffed and ebbed and swirled.

She touched down in her rocket ship
and leapt to desert sand,
as Bee became the first from Earth
to walk the Martian land!

But something unexpected
caught the corner of her eye —
she spotted dusty footprints
leading to a ship nearby.

All bursting with excitement,
Bee then bounded to the door.
It slid aside, her eyes grew wide,
to see what lay in store.

A super-duper spaceship with
a strange, outlandish crew!
A Martian dad, a Martian mum —
and Martian toddler too!

"Hello!" said Bee. "I'm here in peace.
I come from Planet Earth."
Before too long the room was filled
with merriment and mirth.

Her new friends kindly showed her
   all the sights there were to see —

each crater,

pit,

and canyon —

they explored them all with glee.

And when time came to say goodbye,
they handed Bee a gift:
a ruby stone to bring her luck
and make her journey swift.

Bee climbed inside her rocket ship
and heard the countdown start.
She closed her eyes and held the stone
beside her beating heart.

Tick-tock! Bee stretched.
Tick-tock! Bee yawned.
She sat upright in bed.

Her dream had come back home with her,
now racing round her head.

Rushing into Mum and Dad,
Bee told them what she'd done,
about her great adventure
on the fourth rock from the sun.

"Oh, Bee!" said Dad. "You make me proud!
You saw your mission through.
Great courage and ambition
can make all your dreams come true!"

Thinking all about her dream,
Bee wanted to see more,

she longed to visit planets
and new worlds she could explore.

She thought about her Martian friends
and wished they could be real,
then remembered something special
and let out a little squeal.

She dashed back to her room
and found it gleaming in the sun . . .
A ruby stone not of this world,
and hers, the only one!

Now here is Bee about to board
her rocket ship to Mars,
tingling with excitement
for her journey to the stars.

She thinks about the little girl
who made her dreams come true,
through hard work and commitment,
her ambition grew and grew.

She looks down at the ruby stone
set on her golden chain,
determined to succeed
and find her Martian friends again.